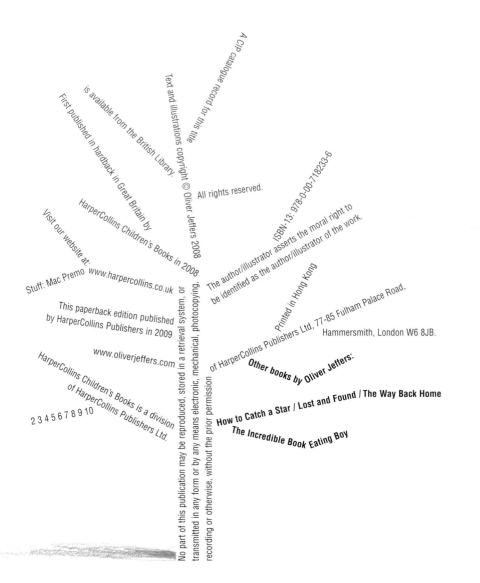

A CIP catalogue record for this title

Text and illustrations copyright © Oliver Jeffers 2008

is available from the British Library.

First published in hardback in Great Britain by

HarperCollins Children's Books in 2008

Visit our website at:

Stuff: Mac Premo www.harpercollins.co.uk

This paperback edition published
by HarperCollins Publishers in 2009

www.oliverjeffers.com

HarperCollins Children's Books is a division
of HarperCollins Publishers Ltd.

2 3 4 5 6 7 8 9 10

ISBN-13: 978-0-00-718233-6

The author/illustrator asserts the moral right to
be identified as the author/illustrator of the work.

Printed in Hong Kong

of HarperCollins Publishers Ltd, 77-85 Fulham Palace Road,

Hammersmith, London W6 8JB.

Other books by Oliver Jeffers:

How to Catch a Star / Lost and Found / The Way Back Home
The Incredible Book Eating Boy

for Cate

the GREAT PAPER CAPER

OLIVER JEFFERS

HarperCollins *Children's Books*

There was a time in the forest...

when everything was not as it should have been.

Everyone who lived there had been noticing strange things.
Branches, they agreed, should not disappear from trees like that.

Someone, they agreed again, must be stealing them
and they each in turn blamed the other.

But they all had a solid alibi which meant it couldn't possibly be them.
So the tree thief must be someone else.

It was all very mysterious indeed.

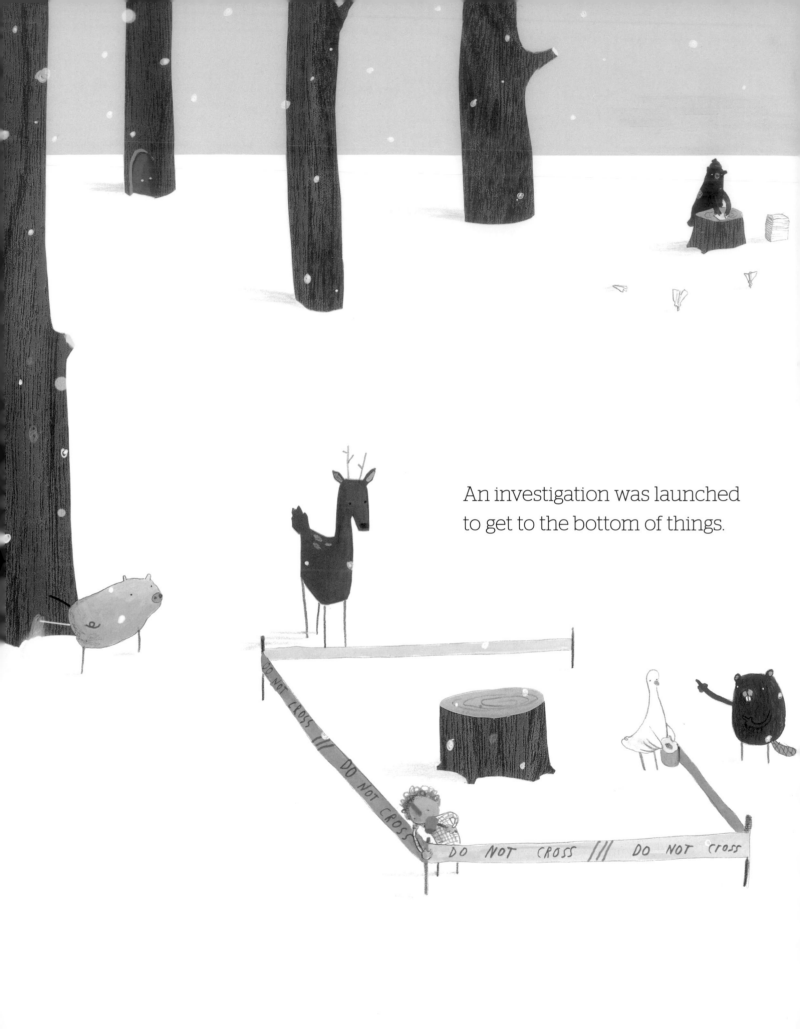

An investigation was launched
to get to the bottom of things.

They were each given a different job to do so the tree thief could be caught.

They took photographs,
made notes and
examined every leaf.

But no matter how
hard they investigated,

no clues could be found.

Then an eyewitness report led them to some
evidence that had blown in not far away

and it had the bear's
paw prints all over it.

They had found their culprit.

The bear was brought in to have his picture taken

9'0"
8'6"
8'0"
7'6"
7'0"
6'6"
6'0"
5'6"
5'0"
4'6"
4'0"
3'6"
3'0"
2'6"
2'0"

NOT me

The next day he confessed everything in court...

all about the paper airplane competition and how badly
he wanted to win, and he knew he wasn't very good,
and he had run out of paper, and he had no one to ask
for help. He was so sorry for taking their trees without
asking, he hadn't meant to do so much harm.

Hmm, well all right, they all thought.
But he'd have to make it up to them by replacing the trees.
And a paper plane competition indeed? That sounded interesting.

The bear kept his word

SEEDS

and made it up to them.

And as the others
helped him gather up
the old paper planes,
they had an idea...

they put them all together and made a new one.

fin